To Eunice McMullen, 18 years and counting...

And a big fat hug for Monika and Luka

HUGLESS DOUGLAS

BY DAVID MELLING

tiger tales

One spring morning, a sleepy someone let out a big yaaawwwwn from the back of a deep dark cave.

It was a young brown bear and his name was Douglas.

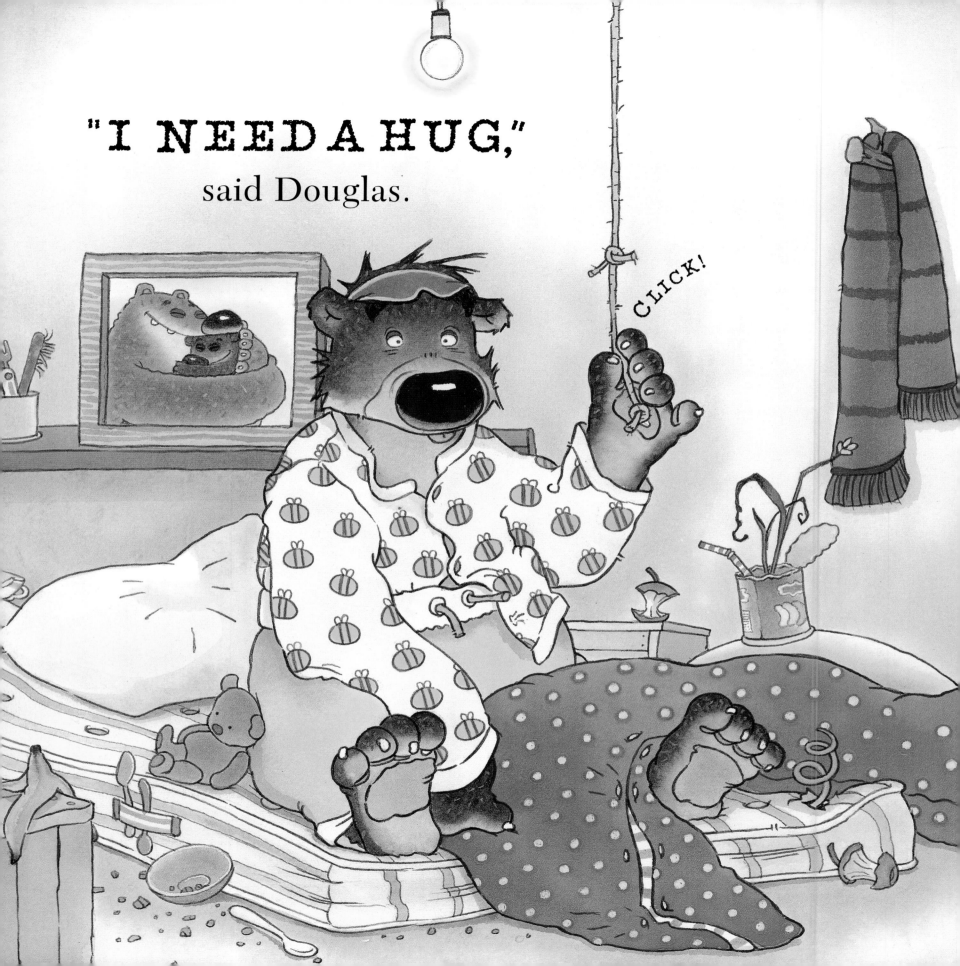

So he wriggled
out of his pajamas,

brushed his hair,

put on a scarf, and went
to look for one.

"My best hugs are **BIG**," thought Douglas. So he went up to the biggest thing he could find, wrapped his arms all the way around, and gave it a squeeze.

It didn't feel right.

"Oof!" grunted Douglas.
"It's a bit...too...

heavy!"

HELP!

"My best hugs are **TALL**," thought Douglas.

So he went up to the tallest thing he could find.

He hugged
the bottom...

he hugged
the middle...

and he hugged
as high as he
could reach.

But it was all wrong. And it gave him splinters.

"My best hugs are **comfy**," thought Douglas and he trotted toward a cozy-looking bush.

He hugged the bush but something felt very odd.
The leaves *quivered* and *trembled*...

and ran away!

"GIVE ME A HUG!" cried Douglas.

"No!" baaed the sheep. "We're too busy."

He scooped up armfuls anyway and tried to cuddle them gently, but they kicked and squirmed and didn't like it at all.

Poor Douglas!

"WHY CAN'T I FIND A HUG?" he said.

"If I want a hug," said a wise owl, "I sit in my tree and—"

"Let me try!" whooped Douglas and he scrambled up next to the owl.

But he soon found himself in a little trouble.

"Whooooo, whoooooo!" said the owl angrily.

"I only wanted a hug," sniffed Douglas. "Perhaps there's one down here?"
He felt something long-eared and rabbity and gave it a tug.

Douglas could tell the rabbit didn't want a hug.
He sniffed again and, without thinking, wiped
his nose on its fluffy tail.

"Excuuuse me!" shouted the rabbit.
"Put me down!"

"BUT I NEED A HUG," said Douglas,
"and I can't find one anywhere."

"Oh, I see," said the rabbit kindly.
"Come with me."

He took Douglas by the paw…

and led him up, down,
and around.

At last they came to a deep dark cave where a sleepy someone was just waking up.

"YAAAWWWWWW

Douglas peeped inside. He had the funniest feeling that he knew the someone very well.

"HUG?" asked Douglas,
and ran as fast as he could
toward . . .

his MOMMY!

"Come to think of it, my best hugs are from someone I love," said Douglas. And he snuggled into the biggest, warmest arms he knew.

Sandwich Hug

Goodnight Hug

Upside-Down Hug

Don't-Let-Go Hug

Falling Hug

Shy Hug

Group Hug

Back-to-Front Hug

Solo Hug

Tummy Hug

Daisy-Chain Hug

Big Hug

Come-and-Get-It Hug

Unrequited Hug

tiger tales

an imprint of ME Media, LLC

202 Old Ridgefield Road, Wilton, CT 06897

Published in the United States 2010

Originally published in Great Britain 2010

by Hodder Children's Books

a division of Hachette Children's Books

Text and illustrations copyright © 2010 David Melling

CIP data is available

WKT1109

ISBN-13: 978-1-58925-098-7

ISBN-10: 1-58925-098-2

Printed in China

1 3 5 7 9 10 8 6 4 2

NOV 17 2010